2020
CORONAVIRUS

Kay Jay

Illustrations by: Sherlena S. Brown

To order additional copies of this book, contact:
Xlibris
844-714-8691
www.Xlibris.com
Orders@Xlibris.com

ISBN: Softcover   978-1-6698-0182-5
        EBook   978-1-6698-0181-8

Print information available on the last page

Rev. date: 11/30/2021

2020 CORONAVIRUS
KAY JAY

New York City (Times Square) was a ghost town. The city that never sleeps. It fell asleep.

In Harlem, (One Hundred twenty fifth street) the people never practiced social distancing.

In midtown, some people walked into the street as if it was no red light or green light. Traffic was light. Rush hour was a breeze.

In the Bronx, some people were cooking out in front of their houses instead of their back yard.

In Mount Vernon, some people were painting bikes in front of their house without a mask or gloves. Meanwhile, someone is smoking in front of the person painting the bike.

In Prospect Park and Central Park, some people were not practicing social distancing cooking out in the park. The groups were at least fifty people.

In Queens and Long Island, I actually saw people following the rules of social distancing.

In the rest of the world, many people lost their lives. This virus was really deadly.

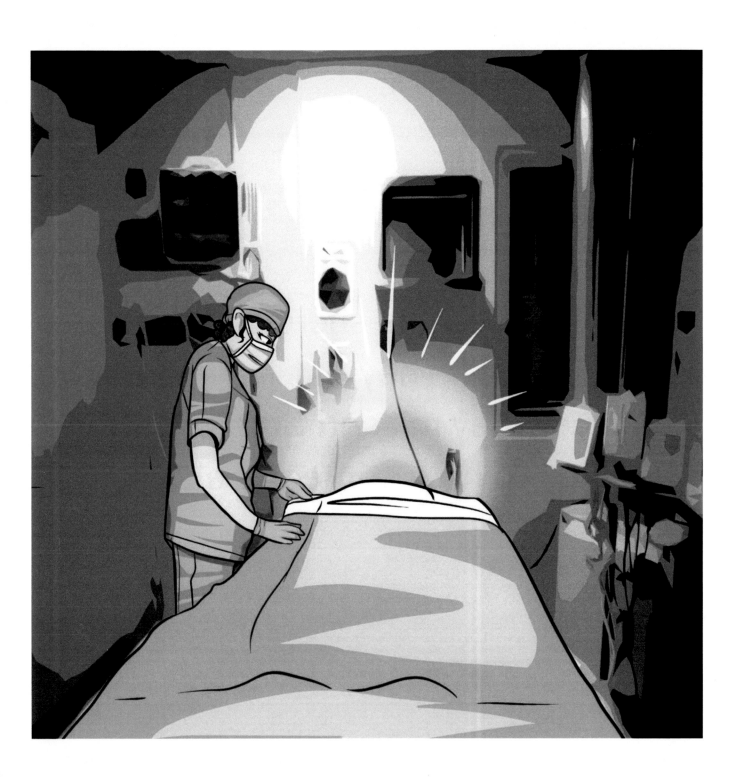

The Heroes and sheroes, they were unbelievable. They put their lives on the line. They missed time with their families to help someone else.

Printed in the United States
by Baker & Taylor Publisher Services